TIMOTHY MEADOWMOUSE

TIMOTHY MEADOWMOUSE

Rita Hanson

To order additional copies of this book, contact:
Xlibris Corporation
1-888-795-4274
www.Xlibris.com
Orders@Xlibris.com
28581

CONTENTS

ALL ABOUT NORMIE

The oldest mouse in recorded mouse history was named NORMIE and he lived in Boston. There was a reason for his long life as you will see as you read this story. He lived more than twice as many years as any of his brothers and sisters.

When his Mother told him he must leave her home and seek a life of his own, he put his few belongings together and said "Goodby." As he stepped out onto the cobblestones of this old city, his Mother said, "Be careful in every thing you do". All that he had heard or learned in his youth was brought to mind. One idea he had heard many times was that in order to eat well one must choose a home of rich folk and one with children—rich folk for lots of food and children for eating all around the house and dropping crumbs.

As he scampered along the cobble stones he saw a group of boys and girls playing in a yard fenced in with wrought iron bars. He stopped abruptly and thought, "This looks like a good place for me". However he must check out the big house to see if there was an entrance for him. He circled the house and was quite dejected. He found nothing. Then on a second tour of the foundation he found a hole between the cellar and first floor. Now, elated, he pushed his little body through the crevice and found himself in the corner of a huge room. In the center of the room was a large table and six chairs.

"Oh boy," said Normie, "This is looking better and better!"

His first job was to make an opening in the side of the entrance. It was a hard job because he had to chew the wood to make enough room for his nest. Outside he found some grass for a rug. Finally he felt at home. It would be a long time before he would mind being alone.

Now, with his work finished, he realized his tummy was asking for some food. He edged out into the great dining room and skipped under the table. There was not a sign of any food. Suddenly, he heard a scratching noise and out from a hidden hole came several mice with the same purpose.

"What are you doing here? said the leader.

"I thought this would be a good house to live in." replied Normie.

"Well, you know, mice are not like many greedy animals. You are welcome to stay and eat with us," said Peter, the leader. "What you must know is that there are very many crumbs under the table but as soon as the family leaves, the maid comes in and cleans everything up with a big machine. We have just a short time to come out and get food. You must listen for the scraping of the chairs and then dash out." Normie thought that this was a little daring but agreed to try.

Soon it grew dark and nestled in his little space he heard much talking and laughter from around the big table. Quickly all of the chairs scraped and the family hastened out the door. At that precise moment a whirling group of mice made a mad dash to clean up the crumbs. There were bread crumbs, carrot bits, potato pieces and cookie crumbs. They were careful to leave a bit of food so that the maid wouldn't get suspicious.

Now, what made Normie so special? He knew about moderation. He had learned never to try anything to the extreme. His success with these meals was due to his ability to scamper home after eating just enough to feel comfortable. All the other s gobbled all they could and were almost too full to run back

One day Normie went out into the yard and found a lovely garden. Many hyacinths formed a little fence and hid him from the house. Lovely lilies made a wall around him. "This will be my summer home," he concluded gleefully.

He returned to his home and soon heard the familiar voices. It seemed strange to him because it was early in the day and still light. Soon Normie heard singing—"Happy Birthday" and then he knew it was not dinner but it was a party. There were several friends there to contribute to the feast under the table. Many, many crumbs of cake descended to the floor along with bits of popcorn and candy. One child dropped a whole piece of layer cake on the rug.

After the children left all the mice raced to the table. Because Normie was a moderate mouse he tried the candy and found it sticky so then he ate cake crumbs and really enjoyed a little popcorn. But as was his nature when he felt comfortably full, he scampered back to his home. The other mice were very greedy. They stayed on and on and ate to extreme. When the maid came in, they were still eating and she saw where their home was as they ran away.

When the head of the house heard about this from the maid, he blocked the entrance of Peter's home and none of them ever saw that big table again. Normie had the entire place to himself.

As he lived to a ripe old age, Normie was always thankful that he had learned about moderation. He lived long and well with his table snacks and the fresh food found in his garden.

TWIG

Many, many years ago when gnomes lived under mushrooms in the woods, there were tiny fairies who could change themselves and others into different forms. Usually, these little beings were good-natured and aided those who wished to be someone else . . . just for a little while . . . to have an adventure.

On the edge of a forest, next to a wooded area, was a pasture. Here all of the little insects lived in harmony. Grasshoppers abounded and would jump as high as they could over blades of grass.

One day something very strange happened. Two fairies were sitting under a bush watching the happenings in the pasture. They turned their heads to listen as a little voice whispered, "How wonderful it would be if I could be a grasshopper and live in the pasture!" The two fairies turned to see who had made the plea. All they saw were some pebbles and a gnarled little twig which had fallen from it's home on the branch above.

The two little fairies grinned at each other. They could help this fellow have an adventure. One of the fairies asked him very seriously, "If we make you into a bug, will you plan to come back here in a period of time and return to your original form?"

"Yes, oh yes!" was the reply. Within seconds a beautiful grasshopper arose from the ground and jumped just as high as he could. As he soared through the air the fairies heard a faint sound, "Thank you, thank you!"

Now, one would think that this was so easy that anyone could do anything that he wanted. But the fairies had not told the new grasshopper that he must repay this favor. In order to return to his original form, it would be necessary to do a good deed for someone else . . . perhaps even give his life.

Many of the grasshoppers in the field saw this large, green hopper with his dark wings and said, "What is your name?" The new grasshopper, feeling very happy and free replied, "My name is Twig!" And he was welcomed into the life of the pasture where he spent much of his time trying to find the tallest blades of grass upon which to jump!

Now, as everyone knows . . . or soon learns, one cannot spend all of his time playing. Twig was sitting on a leaf one day and thought out loud, "I've been having so much fun, perhaps, soon, I should do something to pay back all of my happiness." He thought and he thought but could not think of anyone he could help.

Then, quite unexpectedly, one spring day, clouds rolled in and rain poured down. The raindrops banged on the trees in the forest and gradually the pasture became filled with puddles and streams. All of the grasshoppers and their friends hastened to climb bushes and tall plants to save themselves from a watery death.

Twig, as he was big and strong, sat majestically on a bush near the edge of the forest. Suddenly, he heard a voice crying "Oh, if I could only be a grasshopper, I'd be able to jump out of this big puddle." Twig looked down and swam under the ladybug. He pushed her above the water so she could reach the saving branch. The ladybug was safe but Twig did not come up. He had not known that a grasshopper could not jump if he was wet.

The next day the water receded and puddles dried up. Two tiny fairies were sitting on a bush. They looked down and saw some pebbles and a little twig nestled in the mud. They looked at each other and grinned. One said, "His adventure is finished." As they turned toward the sun a tiny, orange ladybug fluttered over the pasture.

TIMOTHY VISITS THE FARM

O ne early morning Timothy hurried outside to see if the sun had come out. As it was very bright he hastened out the door and ran down to the gate. He wondered which of the paths he should take. He decided to choose the one to the left whose trees were covered with moss and made the path quite dark. Timothy was feeling brave so he turned and walked slowly down the way. Further along the path widened and Timothy saw a large walk leading up to a farmhouse with an old barn next to it. He stopped and then continued on until he reached a fence which was leaning toward the ground. On the other side were a few cows grazing and they didn't even look up to see the tiny mouse.

Suddenly a loud noise echoed from the nearby pasture and a frightened Timothy crouched down. As he looked through a hole in the fence there appeared several roosters and hens heading his way. A scared Timothy stood very still and hoped none of them would see him. But, alas, all of the birds stared at him and became very quiet. One old rooster questioned him, "Who are you and what do you want?" Timothy answered in a small voice, "I am lost. Can you help me?" The many birds crowded to the front and tried to give him some advice but the old rooster, named

Chief, stopped them. "We will help you if you tell us where you came from." Timothy spoke in a low tone, "I took this path and it led me right to your place." Chief listened intently and then in a low voice offered the little mouse some food. Timothy followed them into the barn and looked with wide eyes at all the corn and grain scattered on the wooden floor. At once the birds pecked the feast and didn't stop until their stomachs were full. After some time the eating stopped and all the hens and roosters and chicks again were interested in their little guest. Timothy said goodby to them all and started on his way home.

He felt so comfortable with his tummy full that he decided to have a short nap. His eyes fell on a small bunch of leaves under a great tree and he headed toward the shady spot. There he curled up and was soon fast asleep. This was not a smart decision to make but he had forgotten the most important rule of his life. His Mother had taught him never to go to sleep unless he was at home.

After a few minutes had passed a lean cat sneaked up and stopped a few feet away. The cat watched the tiny meadowmouse and began to smack his lips. Just as the animal was about to jump Timothy opened his eyes and with a gasp he jumped away and ran as fast as he could down the dark path. He burst into the door and raced over to his Mother who grasped him tightly in her arms. Little Timothy in tears told his parent of his terrible ordeal. She wanted to scold him but she felt so sorry that all she could do was comfort him. It was an experience that that tiny mouse would never forget!

NEARLY GOODBY TO TIMOTHY MEADOWMOUSE

"Now, Timmy, you behave yourself and don't get into any mischief" Mother Meadowmouse cautioned him as Timmy grabbed his cap and headed for the edge of the nearby woods.

"Yes, Mother," he squeaked back at her as he disappeared into the thick blades of green summer grass and flowering brambles that dotted the lovely meadowland. He could hear birds in the distant branches singing merrily. Farther away he could hear the muffled sounds of his friend, Benny Beaver, as he swagged away with his large tail, pounding down the mud on the sticks and branches that formed the roof of his den.

Timothy wasted no time in exploring the thickets and blueberry bushes searching for some morsel of food. As he raced about in and out of the tiny clumps of grass, he began to feel a little tired though it was still early in the morning. Spying a soft tuft of grass near a hollow in a log, he decided to stretch out and take a little nap before returning home. Soon Timothy's eyes began to droop as he folded some of the large blades of grass across his chest to make a kind of blanket. He partly hid himself from the unfriendly creatures of the forest. Before he realized it he was sound asleep in the warmth of his make shift bed.

What Timothy had forgotten were the words of his Mother and Dad. First he had not been careful to conceal himself completely. Wouldn't you know? He hadn't escaped the large eyes of Glider, the Owl. In no time at all Glider was moving silently toward him from far above. He was careful not to cast a shadow that might fall across Timothy's face and suddenly wake him.

As he came ever nearer, another pair of eyes saw him. Squeaky, the Squirrel had been sitting in his nest, far above, watching the drama that was happening below. Squeaky lost no time in doing what any friend of the forest would do for Timothy if they could. Squeaky quickly took careful aim and dropped a large acorn right on Timothy's tummy that awakened him with a sudden start. The first thing he saw were the huge wings about to enclose him and the large talons about to seize him. Timothy was scared to death but being a meadowmouse he was very quick in his movements. In a wink of an eye he had disappeared into the hollow at the end of the log! What a close call! Inside the hollow, Timothy's little heart was beating faster and faster. As Glider turned about and flew away madder than a hornet, Timothy began to catch his breath as he let out a sigh of relief at his close call. Very carefully he looked about before he emerged from the opening. In the distant sky he could see Glider disappear into the thick woods.

As he began to run toward home, another large acorn landed nearby and scared him out of his wits. Timothy thought it was another owl that had sneaked up on him. There was Squeaky reminding him of his foolishness in not being careful. "Timothy," his Mother greeted him. "Did you find anything to eat?" "No, I was just looking around." "Well, Timothy, I think the least you could have done was bring home a few acorns". When Timothy heard that his face broke into a big grin!

THE TREE ADVENTURE

Not only was Timothy Meadowmouse a curious mouse but also he was a very brave little animal. Some in his family thought he was being fool hardy. One morning since his chores were done his Mother said that he could go for a walk over to the pasture. Now, Timothy didn't call it a "walk", he called it an "adventure".

As he scampered along the old wooden fence that Farmer Brown had put up many years ago, he met some of his friends. Near the field-stone wall also built by Farmer Brown, Timothy saw Mr. Groundhog peeking out from his covered lair. Closer inspection showed three pairs of beady eyes also checking out Timothy. They remarked about the beautiful day and how clear it was to spot if he were watching near by.

Now past the stone wall and still traveling along the wooden fence, Timothy saw another little snout sticking out from the tall grass. Old Opposum said "Hello" and then proceeded to slowly walk into the pasture. Timothy thought to himself, "Old Opposum is so slow it is a wonder that he has lived so long and not gotten caught."

Timothy slowed down as he came to the edge of the pasture. He stopped and took a long look. Now the excitement of something new grasped him and he shivered all over. He had never been past the wooden fence and now he saw something that he had never seen before. A short distance into the field Timothy saw a huge tree whose branches spread down almost to the ground. He had seen many trees in his young life but none like this. He remembered the tall fir trees on the other side of the hill and the great maples surrounding Farmer Brown's yard. All their branches were high on the trunk. The branches on this tree were bent down so much that the boughs touched the grass. He stopped and crouched down so that he was out of sight as he planned his next move. All his instincts told him not to go any further but his curious nature urged him to go up to the special tree and see what was behind all those angled boughs. He even had a wild idea about climbing up on one of those branches, whose gentle incline made it all seem easy. "If I don't go now, I'll never know about that tree." In a very quiet way Timothy Meadowmouse started across the field gingerly placing his feet so that no crackling leaf or broken twig would give him away.

Now the adventure really began. As Timothy progressed he suddenly was close enough to hear a rapid chirping noise. He had heard that sound once before and that was when the Robin family had had some chicks in a nest high in the maple tree near his home. He wondered what family was hidden in that strange tree. He stopped at one of the boughs and looked in. There, indeed, was a little nest with three little mouths reaching up for food. Usually when there are babies in the nest, one of the parents stays to watch them.

However, because there were such a lot of worms in the ground, both the parents tried to find as many as possible as quickly as possible so as to hush up their noisy children.

Then the beautiful day turned into a horrible fright. Suddenly Glider, the Owl swooped down with every intention to pull Timothy out of the grass and catch him in those powerful claws. In a moment of life saving fate Glider saw the tiny birds in the nest. His greed made him forget how much he wanted Timothy and he sailed over his head and grasped the side of the nest. At that instant two black furies flew into the nest and both together they pecked the owl so fast and hard that Glider raised his wings and disappeared from sight. He was so surprised that he forgot how much bigger and stronger he was and could have succeeded in his dinner search if he hadn't become confused.

Finally when Timothy's heart had slowed it's beating and his mind became clearer, one frightened little mouse started for his home. He wanted so much to tell his family about the ordeal but thought better of it. His mother would be so upset. As he passed Glider's favorite tree he looked up and there was Glider, not the least bit interested in what was going on below; he was soothing his wounds and hoping very much that no one saw that exibition of which he was a part. One must realize that owls are very proud of their size and quickness and Glider felt quite embarrassed about his beating by two little birds.

Now our adventurous little mouse was just about home. He heard his Mother calling to his brother: "If Timothy doesn't come home soon, we will have to go out and find him." That put a smile on little Tom's face because he wanted to leave the nest and see the world.

Just at that moment Timothy ran through the doorway with a yawn as he wanted his Mother to think his walk had been a "ho-hum" type of travel and that nothing of any consequence had happened. All the family were glad to see him and after a grand dinner the young ones, this time including Timothy, arranged themselves around their Mom and Dad and waited for the stories to begin. Before his Mother could decide on what story to tell, Timothy asked "Mom, before the story starts will you tell us about that old tree whose limbs almost touch the ground?" "Oh, you mean the one by itself in the pasture? That tree is over one hundred years old. It was planted long, long ago when Farmer Brown's early ancestors first discovered this beautiful land with the pasture and fir trees. One year there was a terrific storm which became a hurricane. All the trees in the pasture area came down except Farmer Brown's. This tree bent over and placed all its limbs down around the trunk and waited. When the storm was over only one tree remained with its branches leaning down to the earth. It had survived."

After this Mother Mouse jumped up and said "Let me give you some advice: Don't ever go down to that tree because it is very dangerous. Glider the Owl is always near by waiting to catch a little field mouse or a baby chick." After hearing this advice Timothy Meadowmouse shivered and then he smiled. He knew this story first hand!

A PINE CONE'S ADVENTURE

I f you go out to a pine forest and look up in the branches, you will see groups of pine cones—some in small bunches and some in bigger ones. On a particular tree in a small pine forest there were several clusters of cones. They were a family. One of the young cones was very unhappy because he wanted to travel and see how life was on the ground.

One day he asked his father, "Dad, would you let me go down to the ground and see how all the other beings live?" His father answered, "Well, Son, that is a very exciting thought but really it has never been done before. You better not." The little cone went back to his silent wishing and hoping someday it would happen.

During a heavy storm one day the wind blew and blew. "Now is my chance," said little cone and he wiggled and wiggled until suddenly he was loose. Through the air he flew and landed with a bump on the pine needles below. His travels had begun. He should have a name as he goes on his trip. He shall be called Piney Cone or P.C. for short.

In order to go anywhere at all P.C. had to determine his mode of transportation. After several attempts, he discovered he could roll quite easily giving himself little pushes. Off he started and soon found himself out of the pine needles and on to something very green and soft. P.C. had never seen grass before and he relished the soft dampness of the blades.

As he rolled to a stop to gaze at a little mountain of dirt with a hole at the top, hundreds of red ants came pouring out of the opening at the top. P.C. was startled because he had never seen anything like this before from his site atop the tree. The ants busied themselves bringing bits of dirt to raise the mound higher. P.C. watched and whispered to himself, "Aren't they an industrious lot?" They showed P.C. that with a bit of work and much cooperation that a lot could be accomplished.

P.C.'s next stop was in front of a gnarled old tree where there was much business going on. There he saw the working bees bringing home nectar from the flowers. As P.C. sat there a smaller bee flew over and said, "Where did you come from?" P.C. replied, "Oh quite aways from here. Tell me what is going on here." The bee slowly lowered himself onto P.C.'s back and said "I'll tell you. We are a bee colony and we make honey from the nectar of flowers. You see the big bees bringing the nectar to the nest. Little bees like me are security guards. We fly around and make sure that no one steals our honey." P.C. was astounded and thought to himself "First the ants and now the bees. How industrious everyone is." P.C. felt a little bad because as a pine cone he felt that he had accomplished nothing in his life.

Off P.C. started again down a path which led through the field. He noticed as he rolled along that there were very many beautiful insects flying happily around. P.C. had heard of butterflies before but had never seen one.

One very pretty butterfly flew up to P.C. and said, "Welcome to our field and what are you doing here?" P.C. answered, "I'm traveling and learning a lot. Tell me, are you butterflies working or playing?" The butterfly giggled and said "Sometimes things are not always what they seem. You just see us all flying around but actually we are helping the plants and flowers grow."

Again, P.C. was amazed! He began to think seriously of going home. He felt that he didn't belong with all these hardworking insects. "If only I could be good for something," mumbled P.C. as he rolled along heading for home.

Sounds came from the flowers along the garden that P.C. was passing. He drew closer and realized that they were singing. "Oh my", he said, "how happy you are. I wish I could be like you!" The flowers became silent and then one little marigold spoke up. "We are happy because we bring joy to all others with our beauty. Just by existing, others look at us and find themselves smiling and happy." "Would I love to do that" said P.C.

Just as that thought crossed his mind, a big hand grasped P.C. and carried him along. It was dark in the pocket. A lumberjack on his way home was collecting pine cones for decorating a welcome wreath for his front door. After much handling, P.C. was fastened with other decorations to the wreath. The lovely wreath was placed on the front door.

Several neighbors and children came to see the beautiful sight. Some looked up at the pretty pine cone on the top and almost thought they saw a smile. P.C. grinned as much as he could. Now he was good for something! He brought happy smiles to all those who gazed upon the wreath.

THE END

TIMOTHY MEADOWMOUSE SOLVES A PROBLEM

One early morning Timothy woke up and decided to visit his old friend Muddy the Beaver. Because Muddy lived beside the wide creek Timothy had to jump over some slippery rocks to reach Muddy's home. He called to Muddy and heard the answer. "Here I am". Timothy looked around and saw his friend peeking out of his little entrance. Muddy came out to greet him and soon they were deep in conversation. Both of them wanted to give the other all the news that had gone on over the past months.

As the morning went on Muddy and Timothy saw how high the sun had risen and decided to look for some lunch. Our host went inside and brought out a basket of fish which he placed on a flat rock. Soon both of them were busy eating much of the fare. Timothy had never eaten fish before and he was surprised that it tasted so good to him. "May I take a little home with me?" he asked.

Muddy was so pleased that his food had filled up his friend and he answered "You certainly may!" After a short while the two moved out onto the stones and Timothy said goodby to his buddy. It did not take long for him to reach the fence and in a few minutes he was home. "See what I brought home for you," Timothy said. "This is a gift from Muddy. He wanted to show you what he eats for dinner." Mother took the present and passed the fish all around to the brothers and sisters. They were a little cautious at first but it wasn't long before each of them was chewing at a fast rate.

Timothy left them and was again on his way out. He had not gone far when he saw a large animal standing on the path in front of him. He stopped right away and waited to see what the animal would do. Timothy was frightened. Soon the figure moved toward him and slowly looked him over. Then he smiled at the little mouse and said "What is your name?"

"My name is "Timothy" the tiny mouse replied in a very small voice. "Please don't hurt me!"

The huge figure laughed out loud and again smiled at the tiny mouse. "My little friend I would never hurt you. I am a bear and I am lost. My home is a long way far away. Maybe you can help me find my way back." Timothy nodded his head and it was his turn to smile. "Oh yes I would like to help you. What direction did you come from?" The lost bear turned his head to the right side and pointed down the path. "Then that is the way for us to go" answered the bear's new friend. They turned and walked at a good pace and soon came to the edge of the path where it split into two directions. The bear stopped and tried to decide which one they should take. Timothy wanted to take the path that led to the brook because the brook ran in a straight line for a long distance and he thought by following it they would find bear's home. Bear agreed and again the two were on their way. When they came to the brook they quickly turned and began to walk along side. Timothy was getting tired but he didn't want to stop so they kept on going. After traveling for some time the bear saw in the distance his brothers playing together. "I am home" he cried and started to speed up. He was so happy to see his family that he soon reached the place where his parents were standing and they all were so happy!

Timothy beamed and introduced himself. Then he said Goodby and started home. It was quite late when he finally crept in the opening and saw his family who greeted him warmly. They had been worried and now were relieved to see him well and happy. Timothy told them about the bear and again his family was so glad to know that their brother had done a good deed. All the family praised him and now a yawn came from Timothy and it was time to go to sleep.

A tired little mouse was content to fall asleep because he knew that he had again pleased his Mother and Father and the Children.

LRH

TIMOTHY MEETS WHITEY

The day was so warm that Timothy could not wait to go outside and feel the cool breeze blowing. He raced out the door and chose his favorite path. Now it was early in the morning so Timothy headed toward the brook where he knew he could find a place to dip his feet in cool water The brook ran lazily over the small rocks and offered the little mouse a clear spot in which to put his hot feet.

As he soaked in the water he checked all around to see if there was anyone near him who could visit with him. It was very quiet until Timothy heard a voice say: "Do you feel better now?" He turned his head and saw a large bird staring at him. Timothy nodded and smiled as he pulled his feet out of the brook. "Who are you?" Timothy asked. The chicken answered, "My name is "Red Hen" and I live on the farm next to the house up the road. Do you want to come home with me and have some food?" The hungry mouse quickly answered "Yes!", and stood up to follow the friendly bird.

Red Hen and Timothy walked up the path and in a few minutes a large farmhouse came into view. "That is my home" said Red Hen as she pointed to a large door way. They moved a little faster and soon were in the barn looking at a floor covered with corn and other grains. Timothy was so hungry that he bent down and grabbed a fist full of corn and put it in his mouth. Red Hen laughed at him and then joined him in eating the grain. Soon they were joined by many other chickens. All of them seemed in a hurry to eat as much as they could and clean up the barn.

After the eating spree Red Hen moved over to Timothy and asked him if he would like to see the rest of the farm. Timothy wanted to say "yes" but he realized that he must start for home or his Mother would start to worry. He said good bye to his new friends and thanked them very much for the generous meal.

As Timothy hurried along the pasture fence he saw a horse grazing in the field on the other side. He stopped and watched the large animal for a minute and then he decided to talk to him. "Hello" he called out, "Do you know my friend, Red Hen?" The horse turned around and looked down at the little mouse. "Well, well, well" he said, "Where did you come from?"

Timothy looked up at the big creature and smiled. "I live at the end of this path. I am on my way home. Do you live on this farm?"

"Oh, yes, I've been here since I was born. Every day I stay in this pasture and visit my friends and eat this grass. No one bothers me so my days are peaceful and happy."

"You certainly have a great life. I wish that I never had to be scared of others but there are many animals who chase me and try to hurt me."

"Well, any time you want to visit me and be safe, come to my field and we will have a good time together."

"Oh, thank you so much" Timothy grinned and began to stroll down the path "By the way, what is your name? What shall I call you?"

Again his new friend looked down and said, "My name is "Whitey". It will be easy for you to remember because my color is all white."

All the way home Timothy was scampering along. He was so happy to have a new friend who would take care of him. Very soon he reached his home and he ran in and called to his Mother, "Mom, I have a new friend. Let me tell you about him." His mother listened to his tale and was so pleased to know that her son had a new buddy. Timothy took a few minutes to calm down and then related his story again to all his brothers and sisters. They were happy for him. His mother called to them and told them that their dinner was ready so all of the children rushed to the table and mother brought on the big soup dish.

Once again Timothy had come home with good news that his whole family could enjoy.

FRIENDS OF
TIMOTHY MEADOWMOUSE

There never was a time when Timothy wasn't looking for excitment. One morning he left his home and started down the path that was so well known to him. The sun had risen above the trees and brightened the way. Timothy noticed one of his friends sitting under an old oak tree.

"Hi Speedy! Are you waiting for someone?" The brown turtle looked at him and smiled,

"Oh no" he replied, "I'm just resting a short while until I travel to see my family."

"Why don't you walk with me?" Timothy asked.

"You are very kind but I couldn't keep up with you," he answered. The little mouse had to agree but he decided to stay for a short time and chat with his friend. Soon they had to leave each other and Timothy went on his way. Not to far along he discovered another one of his friends who was slowly coming toward him.

"Hi there," Timothy called, "Where are you going so early in the morning?"

"Hello yourself," said Chippy, the chipmunk. "I'm on my way to the creek. The weather is warm enough now to put our feet in the brook."

"Oh yes. Wouldn't that be fun! I'll go with you if it is all right with you. I wasn't going anywhere special"

"Come ahead. We'll have a good time," agreed Chippy.

Timothy turned around and they started toward the creek. It wasn't long before they saw the bubbling brook and both tiny creatures hastened toward it. Soon their little feet were dangling in the water. The excitement grew when a school of tiny fish swam over their toes. Chippy laughed and Timothy pulled his feet quickly out of the brook. He wasn't afraid but he decided that that was enough and both animals again walked up the path. Chippy felt so good after their water adventure that he planned not to go home but to stay with Timothy for a while. They walked at a slow pace until they reached the beginning of the path. Suddenly Timothy stopped and with a big grin offered Chippy a date for lunch. He took him to his home and they were greeted by his family and he asked his Mom if his friend could stay and eat with them.

"He certainly can," she replied, and went to the stove to finish preparing the meal. All his brothers and sisters raced to the table and with a pull Timothy placed Chippy beside his chair. The food disappeared in a very short time and all the little tummies were full. Chippy climbed out of his seat and said that he had to go home but not before he gave a big hug to Timothy's Mother. He waved goodby as he ran and soon disappeared from sight.

It was still early in the day and the sun was high in the sky when Timothy asked if he could go out again. His mother assured him it was alright as long as he was home before dark. As he walked along beside the fence he soon found himself near the pasture where he had met a new friend a few weeks ago. There he saw Whitey. The horse looked up and seeing Timothy he came quickly to the fence "Hello Timothy," he greeted him, and Timothy answered with a smile and soon they were busily engaged in exchanging news about what had happened to each other the past weeks. When it was time to say goodby Timothy started on his way home. He felt so good when he thought of all his friends and the good times they had together. He was, indeed, very lucky.

CHURCH MICE

Everyone knows that there are many, many mice but not everyone knows that there are different kinds of mice—such as field mice, house mice and also a gentler type called church mice. These mice are different from the others because they choose to live in churches where there is not as much food available.

In a little church near the crossroads of America lived a family of such animals. The father's name was "Job" and the mother's name was "Sara" and the two little children were called "Ruth" and "Paul".

One day all the church mice from around the area came together to pray and talk about finding food and having fun. This particular night one of the neighboring mice made a sign for all the others to listen and then he spoke loudly: "Fellow mice, we are in luck! The big church on the main road is having a dinner and service. That means that later tonight we can all sneak in and have a feast. Is anyone interested?" A roar echoed through the crowd. The plans were to meet outside the back rectory door. Ruth and Paul begged their father to let them go with the other older family members.

"Why, yes," said their Father, "It will be a treat for you to see how we fellowship and eat together."

When the moon was high in the dark sky all the hungry mice found their way to the big main Church and scurried down the stairs to find the remains of the great dinner. As Job and Sara entered the room a major picnic presented itself. They both squealed with delight and herded the children into the room. Long tables were all cleared off now but there were many delicacies on the floor and also at the sink someone had cleared several pieces of wedge-shaped cheese from the plates and left them in the sink.

As each anxious mouse prepared to munch on the goodies Job called out, "Wait, we must say a word of thanks to those who provided us with this banquet." And so they did and then the eating began in earnest. It only took an hour or so for all these church mice to completely clean up all the tidbits. When they finished not a speck was left. Job told them all to leave and warned them to be careful and come to the next meeting. Out of the Church poured many mice and headed to their respective homes (churches). All were safe. When Sara had tucked the children in bed they fell quickly to sleep because their tummies were full. Life seemed good to Job and his family.

During the third day of their fasting little pangs of hunger started to come back. Now they began to wonder where their next meal would be coming from. Outside in the back of the church was a large tract of land with many trees on it.

Job said that before it became light he would go into the forest and look for nuts. Just as dawn was breaking Job raced out and gathered a large amount of nuts and grass and returned to his home.

Sara said, "You always provide for us. You are a good husband and father." Job smiled at the compliment and said only to himself that he had a fine family. Once again the four tummies were full and all were content.

A DAY AT THE BROOK

Timothy Meadowmouse was going to take a walk this lovely morning but he wished that he could find a different path to travel on. He is so familiar with all the trails leading into the woods. This time he walked all the way to the edge of the forest and to his surprise he saw a brook that he hadn't ever seen before. It ran along the edge of the wood and disappeared into a large field that was covered with high grass. Timothy stopped and wondered if he should follow along the edge of the brook. He was tempted and as usual his curiosity finally took hold and he continued along the brook until he was covered by the tall grass.

The water ran quietly along until it was stopped by two big rocks that touched each other. In between them there was a small space that looked as though there might be room for Timothy to swim in. There appeared to be a dry ledge on each side of the water so that maybe it was a home for someone. Timothy was not surprised to see a pair of black eyes staring back at him. Almost at once a dark figure emerged and stopped in front of the small intruder. Timothy stared at the sleek wet hair and dark eyes and asked the animal who he was.

"I am a beaver" he said, "and I live here. My name is Benny. What are you doing here? I've never seen you before. Where did you come from?

Timothy answered him in a low voice and told him how he had arrived there by following the brook from its beginning and now found someone to talk with him. The two became fast friends and discovered many things about each other. Benny said that he had never left the brook and had met some friends who came by to see him. He wanted his new friend to stay with him but Timothy said that he must go back the way he came so that he could get home. Benny asked him to come again and visit and Timothy assured him that he would.

On the way home the little traveler finally came to the end of the tall grass and knew the path would soon take him home. When he arrived at his house his Mother wanted to know where he had been all this time and her son told her and his brothers and sisters all about his new friend, Benny. His Mother had worried about him being gone so long but felt better after hearing his story. Timothy was so tired that he could not eat much of his supper and fell sound asleep. His family watched him and then went to sleep too. His Mother smiled to herself and was happy for him.

A BIRD'S LOSS

B linker, a large owl, who was perched on a branch looked down one day to see what was going on in the pasture below. There were four baby foxes playing in the field. They were running about and trying to jump over each other. The largest of the four crouched down and then jumped as high as he could. He landed on top of his brothers. The squealing disturbed all the small animals that were near and suddenly several little beings came out to see what had caused the noise.

Blinker's eyes widened and he pictured that a fine dinner was in store for him. The tiny animals stood motionless staring at the foxes. All of a sudden a low rumble was heard. All the audience scrambled back to their places and only the foxes were left. Blinker prepared to fly down and grab one or two of the frightened babies. The noise that had been heard was from a lawn mower that was approaching them. Before it came too close the hungry bird flew down and attempted to catch a fox. As he opened his claws the foxes dashed into the tall grass and all was lost.

It was not long before all was quiet and Blinker was again resting on his favorite branch. Timothy Meadowmouse was taking a walk and soon found himself near where the little animals had been playing. He saw no one there so he continued on his way and in a little while he came to the edge of the field. Not knowing where he was he kept going toward the woods and soon the familiar path stretched ahead and Timothy smiled to himself. He had found his way home.

Because it was still light he decided to travel further. The path began to twist and turn and came to a small clearing. Timothy heard some noise that became louder as he circled the place. Just a moment later he saw several animals come from the other side. He spoke to them and they all answered with grins on their faces. There were two chipmunks, four rabbits, two turtles, and a large raccoon waiting to hear what Timothy had to say.

"Hello, I'm pleased to meet you. My name is Timothy and I'm on my way home. Can you tell me what this place is?"

The raccoon was the first to speak, "This is our meeting place where we talk and have fun. The sun is starting to get low so we are ready to leave here and go home now."

Timothy felt the same way so he said goodbye and turned around toward the sun and headed for his familiar path. He was home in no time and told of his adventures to his brothers and sisters.

His Mother told him that he must be very careful when he goes on these trips because there are unfriendly animals who might hurt him. Timothy just looked at her because he couldn't believe what she said. Every one that he had met had been so friendly to him. Timothy decided that he would listen to her but keep an open mind when he met new friends.

THE RACE

One day in the magical woods, where fairies dwell, a meeting took place. There were four little beings, all who stopped to talk with one another. A huge black ant, a grasshopper, a big brown spider and a small ladybug made up the group.

They talked about a race. This was the grasshopper's idea because he knew he would win. He knew his big legs would cover a lot of ground. Each of the larger insects smiled inside themselves as they looked at the ladybug. It was so small it wouldn't have a chance they each thought. As they discussed what the prize would be for the winner, two tiny fairies sitting above them on the branch of an old gnarled tree called down to them. "We think a race is a grand idea and we know how to make it more exciting and more fun!!" "Tell us, tell us" came the chorus from the ground.

With wings fluttering, the fairies hovered over the group. "Since we have magical powers, we can grant each of you one wish on how to improve your racing ability to win. However, you must only ask for something you already have on your body." After a little quiet time while each one thought what to ask for, the grasshopper said "My wings are frail but I have very strong legs. Please, make my legs bigger and stronger and I'll surely win." The black ant said "My legs are the strongest and fastest part of me. Please make them tougher and faster." Next, the spider had listened to the requests of his opponents and decided he wanted to be big all over and therefore travel very fast. Now there was just one left—the ladybug. She thought very hard and finally said, "My wings are so tiny but strong. Please give me a great set of wings that won't get tired in flight."

The subject of the winner's reward again took over the conversation. "What is the most important thing in our life?" asked the black ant. "Well, our life itself" replied the spider. "And if I win, I could eat all of you!" "Oh no" said the fairies in unison. "None of you can hurt or touch each other or the race is off!!" "I was only joking" said the spider. "We are all good friends here. What else is important to us?" "Our food" said the grasshopper. "Now that is a good thing" said the ladybug. "The three racers who don't win will bring food to the winner for a month. The winner can rest and not work at all. The reward will be a vacation."

"When you are all lined up to begin, we will grant your requests" announced the fairies. One other decision had to be made and that was the direction and distance of the race. To be fair they asked the fairies to make the rules. They claimed that the race would start in the clearing where they were now and end at the beginning of the wide pasture some distance away. The winner will be the one who steps foot first on the pasture ground. The fairies planned to be there so that an honest decision would be made.

All was in readiness and the fairies waved their wands and immediately the insects were transformed.

Let the race begin!!

The grasshopper took a giant leap and zoomed out ahead of the others. However, the ant and the spider with their huge strong legs soon caught up. The ladybug lifted her wings and flew high above the ground. After the initial start, the ladybug disappeared but no one noticed that because they were watching each other and trying to get ahead. The high stepping legs of the grasshopper continued to give him the lead but the spider and the ant were not to be outdone. Each ran without stopping to rest. It was going to be a very close race.

As they traveled along, the grasshopper jumped blindly ahead. He traveled so fast he didn't watch what was ahead. As he made a high leap, he landed in a berry bush. The thorns held him down and caused him a great loss of time. Eventually he worked himself free but many little thorns annoyed him. With much courage, he jumped again and continued on his way. He did not notice that the spider and the ant had already passed him but soon they were visible ahead racing neck and neck. The ant and the spider weren't looking too carefully at what was in front of them. They both tumbled into a large puddle of rain water. They wasted some time trying to decide whether to go backwards out of the water or swim across to the other side. Then ant continued on slowed down by the water. The spider scooted out and ran around the puddle. He was so happy because he thought he was now in the lead. He saw no one ahead of him.

They came now very close to the meadows edge. The grasshopper again picked up speed and took a final leap. He was in the air and over the pasture but before he came down, the big brown spider leaped onto the grass. As soon as the grasshopper's legs hit the grass, the black ant came across. The three bugs were arguing about who won when one of the fairies called out "What is all that noise? Here is your winner" and they stepped aside to show the ladybug. She was happy and smiling. The grasshopper, the ant, and the spider were amazed. "How could that little thing win?" they asked in unison. "I'll tell you" said one of the fairies. "She made her choice by using her head, by asking for big strong wings that wouldn't get tired. All she had to do was lift herself up and fly in a straight line with no competition or problem." The three losers tried to be good sports and realized that in the future, if a decision had to be made, they must use their brains as well as brawn.

They all thanked the fairies for their help. Then the grasshopper, the spider, and the ant started out to find food for the winner. The ladybug just sat and rested.

TIMOTHY MEADOWMOUSE HELPS A STRANGER

It was a sunny morning and Timothy hurried out the door because he was anxious to see what the day had in store for him. He looked around carefully and then headed down the path which led to the old shallow creek. As he walked along he heard a loud cry for help which sent him quickly to the water. There in the creek was a tiny chipmunk; he had slipped into the creek and was trying hard to stay above the water. Timothy wasted no time in getting to the little animal and he grasped him by his arms and pulled as hard as he could. In no time the small chipmunk was on dry land thanking his rescuer for his life.

Timothy smiled at him and proceeded on his way. As he went further along, the path widened and soon it became a very large field. The sun was high in the sky and it lightened all the stocks of grass and small openings that abounded in the field. Curiosity overcame Timothy and he entered one of the openings only to find that a family of chipmunks had made a home there. He did not want to disturb them so he backed out quickly and took another route.

By this time his stomach began to ache and Timothy knew that the time to eat had come. As he looked about he saw that there was nothing to eat except flowers which he was not accustomed to put in his mouth, He sighed and finally took a small part of a petal and chewed it. It had a sweet taste so he ate just enough to lose the hungry feeling. All the while Timothy could only think of his Mother's wonderful cooking.

He felt now that it was time to go home so he left the sunny field and started back. The sun had traveled toward the West and shadows started to form along the way so Timothy hurried along and soon reached the creek. Now he slowed down and found himself at the family door stop. His brothers and sisters welcomed him and they all asked where he had gone. He mentioned the chipmunk and how he helped him. His family was full of pride and made him recount the story again.

That night his Mother told them about other heroes who had done many great deeds and so all the little mice went to sleep thinking of their brave brother.

THE END

TIMOTHY MEADOWMOUSE
SEES A BIT OF THE WORLD

One afternoon when the family was taking a rest, suddenly, a larger than usual face appeared in the little entrance hole of Timothy's home. All the family were frightened until Mamma Mouse, exclaimed, "Why it is Cousin Runner!" He was given that name because he ran away from home to live in the city. "Please come in," Mamma said "and make yourself at home." The den became a little crowded because Cousin Runner was of a large size as he lived comfortable in his home and never wanted for food.

While the family sat around Runner wove many exciting tales of all his exploits. Little Tom asked his cousin what had happened to his brother who had traveled with him. At this point Runner became quite excited. My brother has become a minister; his name is now "Prayer" and he lives in big Church with his family. I want you all to come back with me and join in the big feast in a few days. Timothy and all his brothers and sisters started begging their Mother to say "Yes" but she knew how dangerous it would be for her to travel with all her little children.

Finally she said "We all can't go but we must send a member of the Family to speak for us." Now Timothy was so thrilled because he knew he was the only one in the family who had gone out of his comfy home. The others were too little and, of course, Mamma couldn't go because she must care for the others. "Would you like to go Timothy?" she asked. Timothy was so filled with excitement that he couldn't answer so he nodded his head. "Alright, that is settled." The next day was filled with plans and Timothy had to pack some food because Runner told him they would not have time to go foraging.

All was ready for the departure and trembling with anticipation, Timothy said "Goodbye" to his Mother and brothers and sisters and stepped out of his home. Timothy liked Runner because he treated him as an equal and not a baby. "Come now", Runner said, "we will cover a lot of our trip in the daylight rather than at night when all the big birds are watching." They traveled along quite speedily past the stone wall and away from the wooden fence. Timothy began to feel a little nervous as he had never been so far from home before but Runner told him not to worry as he knew exactly where he was going and all was well.

Soon the country scene began to disappear and as Timothy strained to see ahead, different types of buildings loomed up on each side of the long street.

"We are almost there," said Runner, "there is nothing to fear now if you stay close to the walls and don't run into the street." For quite some time Timothy followed Runner along side the walls when suddenly Runner stopped.

"Now, Timothy," Runner said "This is the one dangerous move we must make. To get to the church we must cross the street. To do that safely we must wait until it is very quiet and then make a very fast dash. Once in the Church grounds we will be fine."

The two little animals crouched by the wall and waited.

As small noises here and there quieted down, like a flash Runner raced across with Timothy (like a shadow) beside him. In less than a minute the two speedsters were safe in the Church yard.

They made a little noise as they raced over leaves. Suddenly they were surrounded by many church mice; all of whom were Runner's friends. Runner and Timothy were just in time. One of the little church mice stood up in the middle of the group and made an announcement. While he was waiting for everyone to quiet down, Runner explained to Timothy that this was his Brother who was in charge of the Church. His name was "Prayer" and his wife's name was "Worship" The two children were called "Altar" and "Candle" Prayer started his talk, "Fellow Church Mice, we are in luck! The big Church on the Main road is having a dinner and service. That means at about 11 o'clock we can all sneak in and have a feast. There will he cake crumbs, cheese and crackers, and pieces of cookies. The plans are to meet at 11 o'clock outside the back Rectory door.

While Timothy was becoming acquainted with all his relatives and waiting for the party to begin, he met little Candle and Alter. The children begged to be allowed to go with the grownups. Their Father said "Why yes. It will be a treat for you."

Exactly at the appointed time all the hungry mice found their way to the big main Church and scurried down the stairs to find the remains of the great dinner. "Oh look here," called Prayer. "Oh" squealed Worship as she herded her children into the big room. Long tables were all cleared off now but there were many delicacies on the floor and also at the sink someone had cleared several pieces of wedge shaped cheese from the dishes and left them in the sink. As each anxious mouse prepared to munch on the goodies,

Prayer called out, "Wait, we must say a word of thanks to him above for providing this banquet and so they did and then the eating began in earnest. It only took an hour or so for all those Church mice to completely clean up all the tidbits. When they finished not a speck was left. Prayer Mouse said "We must go now." Timothy and Runner were invited to stay with their cousins and they listened to many tales before they closed their eyes for the night.

Soon the time came when Runner and Timothy had to think of returning home. It was difficult to say goodbye to all his relatives and Timothy had such mixed emotions. It was hard to say Goodbye but part of him was anxious to see his own home and family. Runner and Timothy reversed their trip and soon were back to the wooden fence and then running along the stone wall. Now at home he dashed through the opening and excitedly kissed his Mom and hugged everyone. Then he proceeded to tell of all his adventures. Rest assured it was a very happy group.

Runner felt that he should get back home so he said a quick "Goodbye" and started back. Timothy called out a great "Thank you" for allowing him to have such an exciting time in the big City.